Chris d'Lacey ~ Thomas Taylor

FRANKLIN'S BEAR

Crabtree Publishing Company

www.crabtreebooks.com

PMB 16A, 350 Fifth Avenue,   616 Welland Avenue,
Suite 3308,   St. Catharines, Ontario
New York, NY 10118   Canada, L2M 5V6

For Gabriel and Mum

with thanks

C.d'L.

For Ben

(Durston-Thorndyke not Franklin)

T.T.

d'Lacey, Chris.
Franklin's bear / written by Chris d'Lacey ; illustrated by Thomas Taylor.
    p. cm. -- (Red go bananas)
    Summary: Benjamin Franklin relies on a jam-eating stuffed sidekick as he
conducts his experiments on electricity. Includes nonfiction science and
safety information.
    ISBN-13: 978-0-7787-2674-6 (rlb)
    ISBN-10: 0-7787-2674-6 (rlb)
    ISBN-13: 978-0-7787-2696-8 (pb)
    ISBN-10: 0-7787-2696-7 (pb)
    1. Franklin, Benjamin, 1706-1790--Juvenile fiction. [1. Franklin,
Benjamin, 1706-1790--Fiction. 2. Inventors--Fiction. 3. Teddy
bears--Fiction. 4. Lightning--Fiction. 5. Electricity--Fiction.] I. Taylor,
Thomas, 1973- ill. II. Title. III. Series.
    PZ7.D6475Fra 2005
    [E]--dc22
                        2005016760 LC

Published by Crabtree Publishing in 2006
First published in 2003 by Egmont Books Ltd.
Text copyright © Chris d'Lacey 2003
Illustrations copyright © Thomas Taylor 2003
The Author and Illustrator have asserted their moral rights.
Paperback ISBN 0-7787-2696-7
Reinforced Hardcover Binding ISBN 0-7787-2674-6

Dear Children,

This is a story about a famous bear.
A teddy bear.
His name is not known.

He lived in the house of a great inventor,
around the year 1752.

Some people might try to tell you
that teddy bears were not discovered until
many years later than 1752.

Some people have much to learn . . .

THE STORM

It is nightfall at the house of Benjamin
Franklin, the famous inventor, philosopher,
and scientist. Outside, a terrible storm is
forming. Black clouds roll across the sky.
A rumble of thunder rattles the windows.
Dead leaves rustle and dance on the porch.

5

It is a time when any sensible inventor would be closing the curtains and snuggling up to his faithful bear. Here is Benjamin Franklin's bear. All afternoon, he has been busy in his corner, making a kite from cedar wood and silk. Making things is the bear's favorite hobby – apart from eating jam, of course.

Is it dinner time yet?

But as the sky begins to growl, he puts
down his kite and places two cushions over
his ears. He does not like the boom of
thunder. It make his stuffing wobble.

Suddenly, the master enters the room.
"Come, Bear!" he cries. "There is a great
storm blowing. We must ride and study it."

Quickly, he sweeps the bear into his arms.
Together they leap on to the master's horse
and gallop off into the face of the wind.

The bear does not think much of this.
It is cold and the rain is wetting his snout.
What's more, if he's not mistaken, the sky
is about to be lit by . . .

It's cold!

LIGHTNING!

The master whoops and raises his hat.
"A-ha! Electric fire!" he cries. (This is what
he calls a lightning flash.)

Just then, another lightning bolt zings
through the air like a great blue tongue.
It crackles and dances over the town.

Frraappp! A building bursts into flames.

The master's horse rears up in fright, nearly pitching the bear to the ground.

"Disaster!" Benjamin Franklin cries. "Jeremiah's store is struck and burning."

"JEREMIAH'S!" cries the bear. No, it can't be? Jeremiah's is the place where the master buys jam . . .

Hold on tight, Bear!

A Great Experiment

It is a true disaster. By morning, the store has been burned to a crisp. Everything destroyed. Boots. Clothing. Jam. The lot. The townsfolk fall to their knees and wail. The lightning is the wrath of the Lord, they say. They pray that their homes will not be burned next.

Meanwhile, in Benjamin Franklin's house,
the bear is very worried. It is Friday, the day
the master goes shopping, and there is no
jam on the kitchen shelf. With the store
burned down, what is going to happen?

The bear decides to look in the pantry.
Surely the master has a jar in there? But
the pantry door is firmly locked ...

. . . and the key is not in the biscuit barrel. What has the master done with it? Lost it down the back of the sofa, perhaps?

At that moment, Benjamin Franklin appears. Lo and behold, he has the pantry key. But why has he tied it to the bear's new kite, with a great long length of hempen string?

'Tis missing!

This is why. The master sends the kite
high into the sky. Up it soars, bucking and
flapping. It slices through the sheeting rain.
The pantry key dangles near the end of
the string. The bear stares longingly at it.

His tummy is rumbling like a little volcano. He is hungry. He must have jam. Surely the master will not mind if he slips back home and unlocks the pantry? He begins to reach a hopeful paw to the key.

Suddenly, lightning strikes the kite! It travels down the wet string quicker than the eye can possibly see. Its ferocious energy turns the key blue!

"STOP!" cries the master. He pulls the bear back and hugs him tightly. "You must not touch the pantry key. 'Tis very dangerous.

Waah!

WATCH OUT!

The electric fire has passed along the string and transmitted its energy into the key. If thy paw was to dab the key now, the electric fire would jump into your stuffing and frazzle you, just like Jeremiah's store. All thy fur would stand on end."

The bear gulps. His fur stands on end anyway!

The master gives a satisfied nod.

"The experiment has been a great success. We have shown that the electric fire may flow like water. We must now learn how to make it flow safely away from our houses to save them from its terrible power."

The bear claps a paw across his eyes. "But, Master, what about my jam?"

THE LIGHTNING ROD

Back at home, Bear digs out all the old jam jars he can find. Surely one must contain a smidgen of jam? He rubs his paw around the rim of a jar, hoping to find a tasty streak. To his surprise, a strange hum rises out of the glass. The bear rubs more jars and plays a little tune …

At this point, the master strolls in. He smiles and hums the tune back to himself.

"Very soothing, Bear. A most hummable melody. Have you a name for this musical invention?"

The bear shrugs modestly. "I call it . . . a Jarmonica, Master. Please may we take it to the market square? If you play it, I will dance and beg for jam."

The master shakes his head. He sits the bear kindly on his knee. "Bear, all inventions must benefit mankind. We cannot always be thinking of our stomachs." He gives the bear's pudgy little tummy a prod.

As he does so, a bell mysteriously tinkles. The bear jumps in surprise. "Master, I have bells inside me!" he says.

The master laughs heartily. He gives the bear's ear a loving tweak.

"Not so, Bear. What you hear is my storm detecting system."

He points to an arrangement on the far side of the table.

"That wire runs away to the attic," says Benjamin. "It joins to a spike of metal which I have fixed in place where the pigeons make their nest. I call this spike a lightning rod.

When a storm is near, the electric fire will
energize the rod. Its force, which I now call
electricity, will draw the brass ball towards
the bells, making them do a little tinkle.
This way, we will know when a storm
is coming."

23

The bear gulps and crosses his legs. The thought of more storms is enough to make him do a little tinkle.

Will our house look like the store, Master?

"But, Master," he asks, "what if the wire brings the fizzy-wizzy fire?" He points through the window at the heap of black timber that once was Jeremiah's store.

The master wags his finger. "I have pondered greatly on this. Electricity is a wondrous, natural force. You must be careful of it, Bear, but not so fearful. I foresee a time when it might be made . . . not high in the clouds . . . but here, in our homes, within a small container and only poured forth when its power is needed . . .

Like this, Master?

Nay, Bear, a teapot is far too grand.

. . . come, look into the future with me.

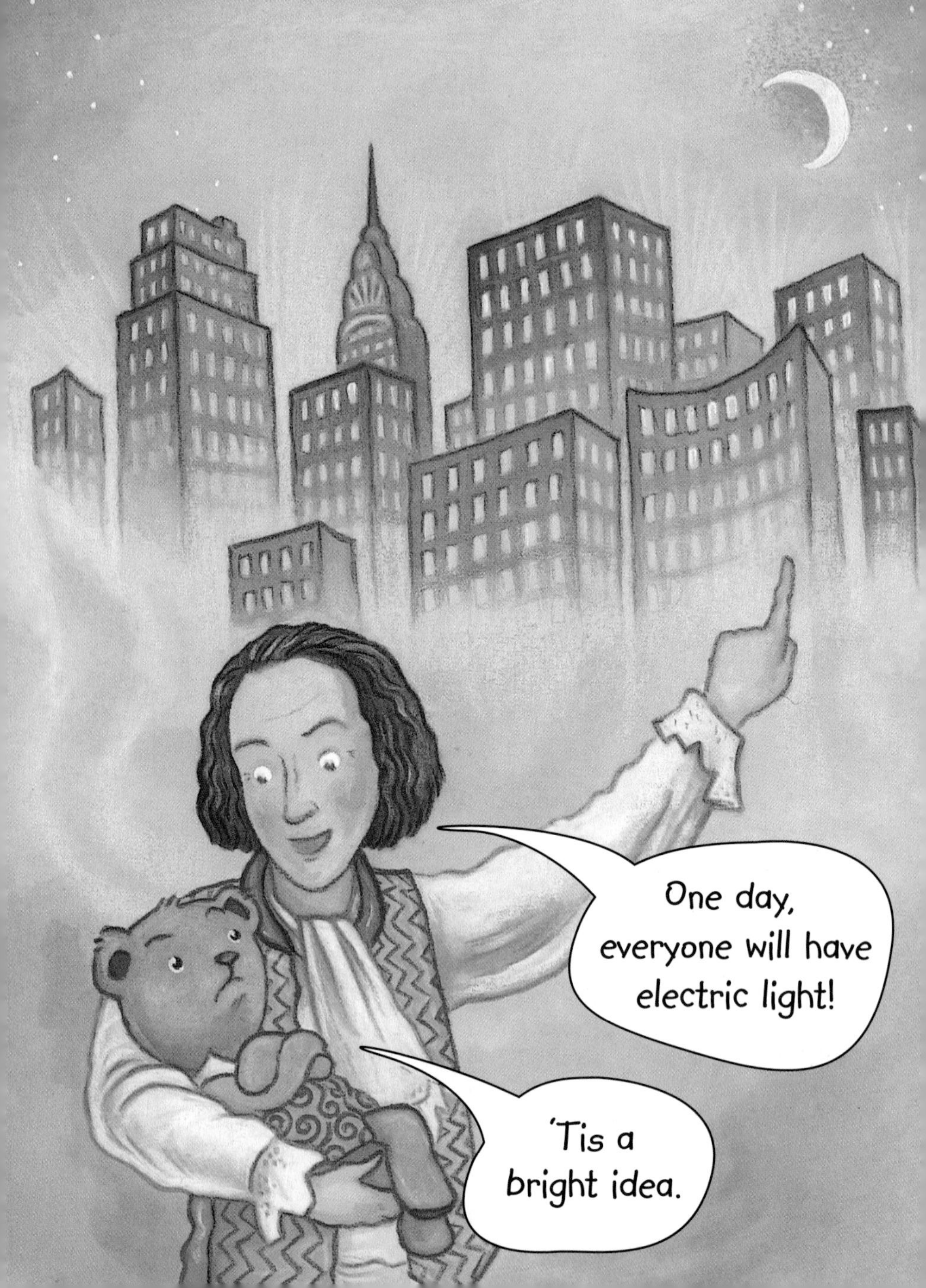

The electricity will flow from something called a battery and will travel around a loop of wires such as this. If a light is placed within the loop, it will glow when the energy passes through it. I also predict that the wires might cover many hundreds of miles.

They might hang in the air . . .

. . . or even be laid in the ground."

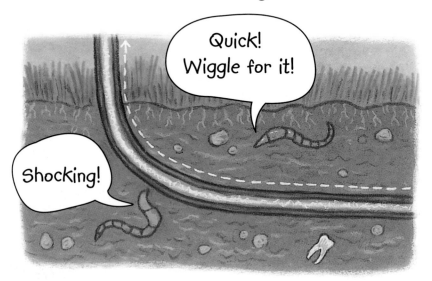

"But, Master," asked Bear "what if the electrickery frazzles the squirmy wormies?"

The master smiles. "Bear, thy stuffing is filled with kindness. Fear not, the electricity will harm no worms. It will flow safely into all our houses and many machines will be worked by it. Lights will be lit, washing be done, food be chilled, bread be toasted . . ."

The thought of toast almost makes the bear swoon. He frowns and paws his snout in thought. Maybe the electrickery could be helpful after all?

He is pondering how to make some useful devices when the storm bells tinkle loudly. More thunder is on the way . . .

THE CHURCH IS SAVED

Within minutes, a howling wind grips the
town. Shutters clatter. Fences lean. Jeremiah's
fluffy black cat begins to look like a pointy
arrow. The heavens snarl. Thunder pours
forth like a giant, burping. It seems to be
gathering over the church . . .

The people gasp in horror. Who can protect their place of worship from the awful electric fire?

Benjamin Franklin – and Bear!

Look! It's Bear and his friend.

Fear not!

"Bring a ladder!" the inventor cries to the crowd. "I must attach this rod to the spire. Quickly, before the lightning comes. The rod will guide the lightning to earth, where it will safely fizzle out. The church shall not be burned."

Daniel Crumb, the farmer, brings a ladder. He lays it against the wall of the church. But the ladder will not reach the top of the spire. And the storm is growing worse. What can be done?

Benjamin Franklin racks his brain.

Hmm! I wonder?

"Bear!" he cries, "you must fly to the tip of the spire and nail the lightning rod in place."

From his saddle bag, he takes out the kite. He ties the bear to it and hands him the rod, a reel of wire, and a good, strong mallet.

Then he rides into the wind until the kite sails skywards.

Up flies the bear –

Waah!

CLUNK! – into the spire.
He scrabbles and hangs on
tight. Were it not for his
velvety pads, he might
be following his mallet
to the ground.

His mallet? Oh
no! Now how will
he fix the rod to
the spire?

clunk!

With pigeon droppings!

Quickly, he gums the rod in place. Then

he slides down the
spire and onto
a ledge. He must
not fall, but he
must escape. It is
dangerous here.
More lightning
bolts are about to
strike. But how can the bear get down?

"JUMP!" cry several voices together.
The bear covers his eyes ... and jumps!

39

He lands safely on the blanket . . . and
bounces into the arms of Jeremiah.

A great hurrah goes up. The bear is safe.
But what of the church?

FRAZ-ZACK!!

Fzzztt! Lightning fizzes from the clouds.
It strikes the lightning rod and flows down
the wire and away safely into the earth.

The people clap and cheer. They raise
the bear onto their shoulders. They call him
a hero and ask him to name his reward.

"We accept nothing," says Benjamin
Franklin. "Our
inventions are
free, for the good
of all men."

But the bear
has other ideas.

Blowing pigeon feathers from his snout he asks, "I don't suppose you have any jam?"

The people mutter amongst themselves. The farmer, Daniel Crumb, steps forward. "Bear, we have no jam," he says. "Would you take this instead?"

He produces a straw-colored pot.

The bear's eyes flash like lightning bolts. Can it be? He dips a hopeful paw. Yes, it is. Scrummy yummy HONEY!

Scrummy honey for my tummy!

Can you imagine what life was like without electricity? We could only dream of what it could be used for.

Today, electricity is used to power many things at home o in school. It can make things . . .

light up . . .

get hot . . .

make sound . . .

or move.

Can you think of other things that use electricity?

Anything which plugs into an electrical outlet uses electricity.

ELECTRICITY IS VERY DANGEROUS.

An electric shock from a wall socket could kill you.

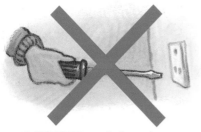

NEVER stick scissors, pens, fingers, or anything else into an outlet.

NEVER touch switches or plugs with wet hands.

NEVER use electrical equipment near water.

ALWAYS remember to hold the plastic part of the plug when you plug or unplug it.

REMEMBER, stay away from electricity outdoors.

It's important to learn to use electricity safely.

ALWAYS ask an adult to help you with electrical devices.

It's too dangerous to experiment with lightning or electricity. But there is a safe form of electricity called "static electricity" that can be produced by rubbing two objects together. Here's a simple experiment.

WHAT YOU WILL NEED:

A balloon   A wool sweater   A wall

1. Ask an adult to blow up a balloon.

2. Then rub it briskly on your wool sweater.

3. Now put the balloon against a wall and let go. What happens?

Remember deflated or broken balloons are dangerous. Dispose of any broken pieces safely.

Franklin invented BIFOCALS by cutting two pairs of glasses in half and putting half of each lens into a single frame.

BIFOCALS

LIGHTNING ROD

He made the LIGHTNING ROD which protected buildings from lightning damage during great storms.

Franklin produced a type of IRON STOVE which warmed homes less dangerously and with less wood.

IRON STOVE

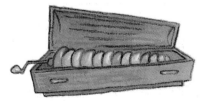

ARMONICA

And he also invented the ARMONICA. It was played by rubbing the edge of spinning glass bowls with damp fingers.

Now it's your turn to make an instrument.

WHAT YOU WILL NEED:

8 drinking glasses of the same size and shape

 A jug of water

A metal spoon

1. On a flat surface, place the glasses near each other, but not touching.

2. Fill each glass with different amounts of water.

3. With a spoon, tap on each glass. Can you hear different sounds?

4. Then, tap on different parts of each glass. What can you hear?

5. See if you can work out how to play a simple tune.

ROH